BARTO TAKES THE SUBWAY

BARTO
TAKES THE SUBWAY

Written by
BARBARA BRENNER

Photographs by
SY KATZOFF

ALFRED A. KNOPF : NEW YORK

L.C. Catalog card number 60–13023

THIS IS A BORZOI BOOK,
PUBLISHED BY ALFRED A. KNOPF, INC.

A NOTE ON THE NEW YORK CITY SUBWAYS

I.R.T. stands for Interborough Rapid Transit. This is the oldest of New York subways. It was built in 1900.

B.M.T. stands for Brooklyn Manhattan Transit. This subway was built in 1913, and has 156 stations on its line.

IND. is the Independent Subway System. This is the newest and longest of the New York City subways.

Last year over one billion passengers rode the subways in New York.

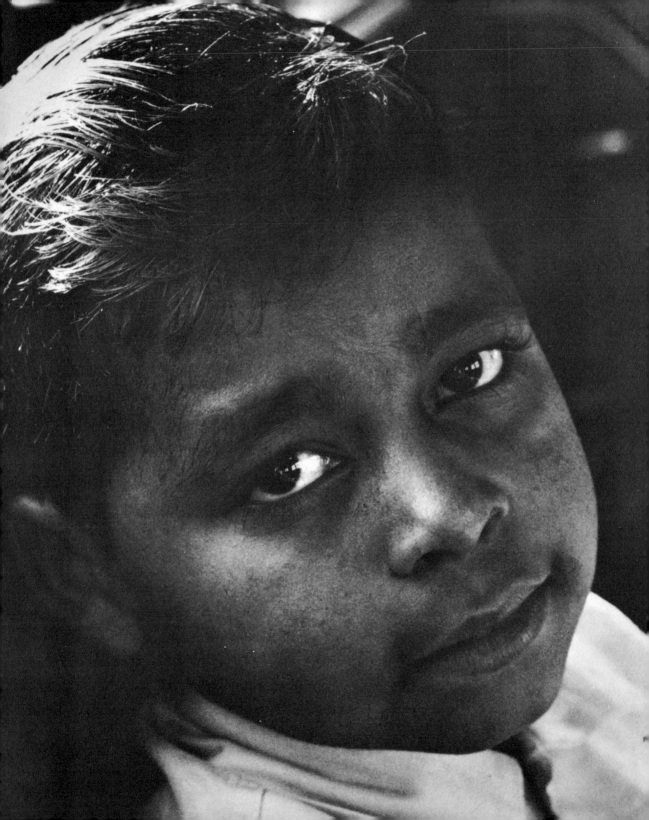

This is Barto Garcia.
He and his family live in New York City.
They came here from a farm on the island
of Puerto Rico one year ago.

What's it like for Barto, living in a big city?
Well, I'll tell you. . . .

It's busy!
The stores are busy.
The pushcarts that sell fruit are busy.
The stands that sell fresh fish are busy.
The ice-cream man is busy. Busy, busy city.

It's noisy, too!
Big boys shout. Girls scream and chatter—
Bang! goes the backfire of a truck.
Honk and toot go car and bus, cab and truck.
Noisy, noisy city.

Even under the street there's noise.
Rumble, rumble under the street.
What's that noise? Barto sometimes hears it when he's
outside playing. It shakes the ground, and if he looks down
through the grating, he can see something whooshing by.

Barto knows what it is—it is the SUBWAY.

The big noisy subway in the big noisy city.

People have told Barto about the subway. He has heard
of the fast train that goes under the ground, but he has never
been in a subway. He has had many rides in a car.

He even rode in an airplane when he came to New York.

But—he has never had a ride on the SUBWAY.

He dreams of riding in the fast subway train.

One day when Barto is outside playing he hears his Mama call,
"Barto, Barto, *ven aca!*"

When he gets upstairs, she tells him, "I have a surprise for you!
You are going with Julie on the subway to visit Grandma."

He hurries to get ready. Clean shirt. Clean pants.
Slick hair. Shiny shoes.

He waits while Mama combs Julie's curls. He listens carefully
while Mama tells him how to behave.

He kisses the baby good-by.

Off they go. Barto feels very grownup as they walk
down the street, until they come to the entrance to the subway.

There is a long flight of stone steps.
One step down. It's getting darker.
Two steps down. Still darker.
Three steps down. Wall of shadow.
Down and dark until. . .

They are under the street
in a big room with shiny walls,
and many signs, and crowds of people,
and a cool, night-time feeling.

People hurry by.

Barto says, "I wonder why they put the subway way down here."

"Because there's no room left up there," Julie tells him.
"The city is too crowded. Too many cars and trucks and buses.
There's no room there for miles of tracks."

And the subway train in the distance seems to rumble . . .
no room, no room, no room. . . .

There is a man down here in the station who sits in a little cage.

"That's the money man," says Julie.

"You mean he gives you money?" Barto asks.

"No, no, this is where you pay for your ride on the subway."
Julie gives the man a quarter and a nickel. The man gives
Julie two round little coins called tokens.

People hurry by.

Barto is in a hurry too. He wants to get to the train.

He tries to go through the turnstile. He pushes and pushes.

"What's the matter here?" Barto asks.
"Silly! You must put the token in the box," says Julie.
Barto drops the token in. Magic!

Now they are on the platform.
There is the long metal track. But where
is the train? Do you hear that rumbling noise? It's coming.
Closer.
Bigger.
Louder.
Closer, bigger, louder.
RUMBLE, ROAR, WHOOSH!
It's gone.

"WHAT WAS THAT?"

"That was the express," says Julie. "Some trains only stop
sometimes. They're express trains. Some trains stop at every
station. They're local trains. That's what we want.
We want the local."

"But trains have other names too," Barto remembers.
"I have seen the letters. Some trains are called IRT. And some
trains are called BMT. And some trains are called IND."

"Yes," laughs Julie, "and this train is called
Lexington Avenue IRT!"

While he waits for the Lexington Avenue local, Barto
looks around. He sees all kinds of machines.
He sees a juice machine.
He sees a weighing machine . . . a soda machine . . .
a candy machine . . . an ice-cream machine!

He looks through his pockets. Only two pennies. Well . . .
One piece of candy can be shared by two. And . . .

"Look, Julie. Sixty pounds!"

They hear the rumble of another train.
People hurry hurry.
The wheels of the train
seem to say hurry hurry,
and the sounds bounce around
getting louder and louder.
Barto holds his ears
as something comes THUNDERING
INTO THE STATION, SLOWS DOWN...
and then EEEEEEERK! It stops.
It's the local.

This is the moment Barto has been waiting for.
CHAAAAH! says the train. The doors open.
But suddenly—people rush out, brush past, hurry by, push, shove,
elbow—everything is happening at once. The train is so big
and black and noisy.

Just for a second, Barto thinks, "Do I want to get into this
big old noisy train?"

"Let's go," says Julie, and she gives Barto a little shove.
CHAAAAAAA! The doors close. Barto and Julie are inside the train.
The train is inside the tunnel. Inside Barto there is a funny feeling!

The train pulls out, jam-packed with people—people sitting, people standing, people reading the paper and people dozing. People are all packed in together, like beans in a pot.

Where is everybody going?

Some people are going to work, and some people are coming home from work. Some people are going visiting, or to the movies, or to the beach. They can go anywhere in the city on the subway.

The big black train roars through the long black tunnel.
Barto holds on to a pole to keep from falling.
Then the train slows down and stops at a station.
People hurry off, and people hurry on.
"Do we get off here?" Barto wants to know.
"No," says Julie, "we have a long way to go."

Again the big black train roars through the long black tunnel.
Finally there is a seat near a quiet nun.
At the other end of the subway car, someone waves to Barto.
"Well, look who's here. A friend from school."

"Where are you going?"

"To my Grandma's. Where are you going?"

"To my Grandma's!"

"That's funny!"

"Let's read the signs for awhile. That one says something about headaches. That one says to drink lots of milk, and . . . hey, there's one I know from school. . . ."

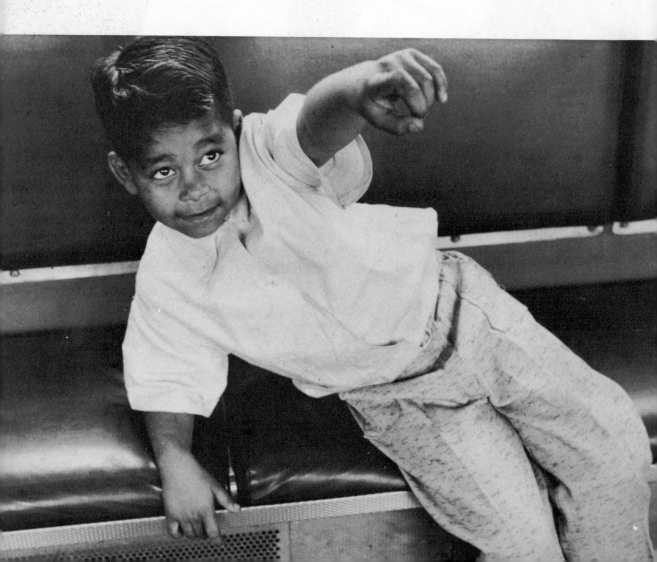

" 'Cross at the green, not in between.' "

Barto's friend gets off at the next stop.

"Julie, when do we get off?" Barto asks again.
"We still have a long way to go."

"I wonder what will happen if I turn this. Maybe I can make the sign say *Express*."

"Barto!" Julie speaks sharply. "Remember what Mama said. Behave yourself."

Barto sits quietly as the train shakes along. Then, all of a sudden, out of the window he sees ...BLUE SKY! They have come from the dark into the light.

Barto looks up and sees into the windows of the houses. He looks down and sees all the trains in the railroad yard.

"*Mira, mira,*" shouts Barto, forgetting to speak English
because he is so excited. "How did this happen? First we were
under the street, and now we are up in the air." Julie explains.
"My teacher says that long ago when this subway was built,
there was no city way uptown here. This was still all farm land.
As in Puerto Rico, remember? Lots of green things growing,
and cows and goats, and no tall buildings. There was plenty
of room. So they put the subway up here."

"Now come," says Julie, "I want to show you something."
They go to the front of the car, where there is a little
round window. Julie gives Barto a boost and then . . .

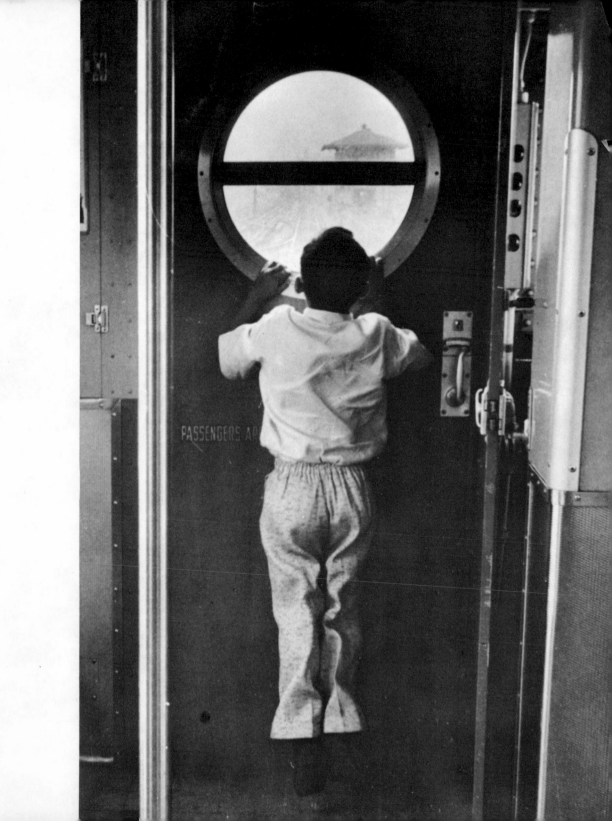

He can see everything!

He sees the tracks, and the signal light that tells the train
GO. STOP.
He sees a trackman, in a cap, fixing
something on the track.
He sees the house where the towerman sits and pushes buttons
that can make the trains go slow, or go on to another track.

Far down the track there is a train coming.
Closer. Bigger. Closer. Louder.
It looks as if it's coming on the same track!
It seems to be coming straight at Barto and Julie.
Will they smash?
Will they crash?
Of course not.

What a relief! Barto swings through the almost empty train,
making believe it is his train, and that he is the conductor.
He calls, "Next stop Cypress Avenue, next stop
Pelham Parkway," all in a deep, loud voice.

"The next stop is our stop," says Julie.
"Oh, no, not so soon!"
Now that it's time to get off, Barto hates to leave.

But the next stop is the end of the line.
Barto takes one last look around, and then . . .

What's behind this door, he wonders. All he can see is
somebody's ear. "It's the motorman!"

Barto watches the motorman pull the handle that makes
the train go slow, or fast, or stop, or start. Then they are at
the last stop, and Julie is calling to him to come.
One very last look and . . .

"Hey, kid." The motorman is calling Barto.
"What's your name?"
"Barto Garcia."
"You're a fine big boy."
"Yes, sir, I weigh sixty pounds."
"I have a boy just about your size," says the motorman.

Then the motorman points to his seat and says,
"How would you like to sit up here for a minute?"
"Boy, would I!"
Before Barto knows what's happening, he's sitting in the little
room that is called a cab, in the seat that belongs to the motorman.

Finally the conductor comes through the car, calling,
"Last stop. Everybody out."
"Come on, Barto," says Julie.

Barto thanks the motorman, and climbs slowly down
from the little seat. Julie is waiting.

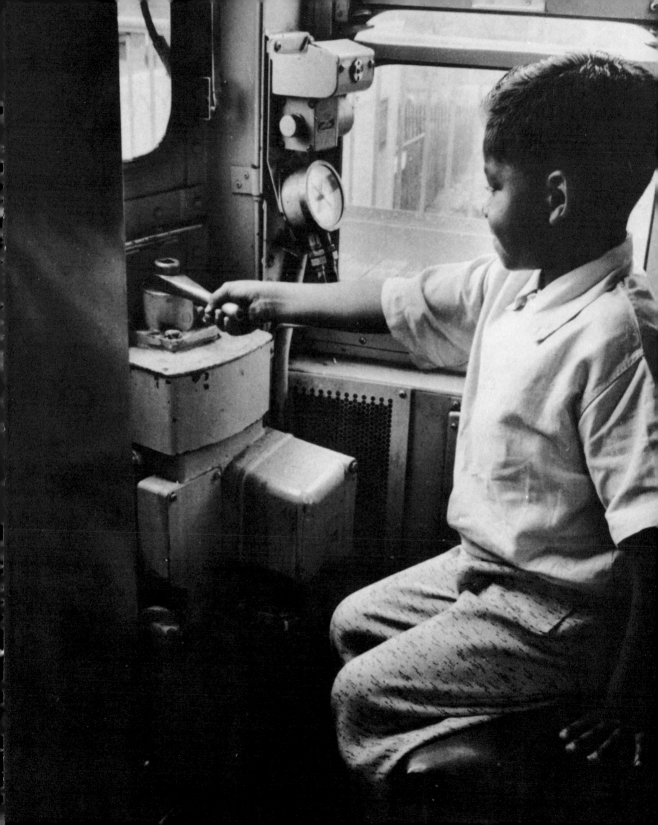

They step off the train. The motorman follows. He walks
along the platform to the very last car of the train. There is a
cab there just like the one in the front. He gets in.
CHAAAAH! The doors close. Slowly the train begins to move—
the other way! The back has become the front, and the front
has become the back.
"They don't even have to turn it around," exclaims Barto.

Barto watches the train get smaller and smaller. He hears the rumble get softer and softer. He is sad.

"Barto, don't be sad," Julie says. "We will go home on the subway, too, you know!"

Of course. There'll be another chance to ride on the train.

"Hurray!" says Barto.

He and Julie race along the platform, down the steps to the street, and up the street to Grandma's house.

They burst in at the door, laughing and talking. "Grandma, Grandma," shouts Barto, "wait 'til you hear about the SUBWAY!"